Leo's
New Pet

First published in 2006 by
Franklin Watts
338 Euston Road
London
NW1 3BH

Franklin Watts Australia
Level 17/207 Kent Street
Sydney
NSW 2000

A CIP catalogue record for this book is available
from the British Library.

ISBN 978-0-7496-6891-4

Series Editor: Jackie Hamley
Series Advisor: Dr Hilary Minns
Series Designer: Peter Scoulding

The author and publisher
would like to thank Robert
Kearney for permission to use
the photograph on page 4 (top).

Printed in China

Franklin Watts is a division
of Hachette Children's Books,
an Hachette Livre UK company.

Leo's New Pet

by Mick Gowar

Illustrated by Richard Morgan

W
FRANKLIN WATTS
LONDON•SYDNEY

Mick Gowar

"My daughter Frances had a hamster called Peanut who escaped. He was coaxed back into his cage with peanuts!"

Richard Morgan

"I hope you enjoy reading this story as much as I enjoyed drawing Leo and his dad looking for that cheeky hamster."

Leo had a new pet –
a tiny hamster.

He didn't have
a name.

"We'll give him a name
tomorrow," said Dad.

"We'll see him in the morning," said Dad.

"He's gone!" said Leo.

"Is he behind the TV?"

"No," said Leo.

"He's under the sofa."

"Call him," said Dad.

"But he hasn't got
a name," said Leo.

"Will he come
out for a carrot?"

"No," said Leo.

"Let's try peanuts,"
said Leo.

"I know what to call him," said Leo.

"Peanut!"

Notes for adults

TADPOLES is structured to provide support for newly independent readers. The stories may also be used by adults for sharing with young children.

Starting to read alone can be daunting. **TADPOLES** helps by providing visual support and repeating words and phrases. These books will both develop confidence and encourage reading and rereading for pleasure.

If you are reading this book with a child, here are a few suggestions:

1. Make reading fun! Choose a time to read when you and the child are relaxed and have time to share the story.

2. Talk about the story before you start reading. Look at the cover and the blurb. What might the story be about? Why might the child like it?

3. Encourage the child to reread the story, and to retell the story in their own words, using the illustrations to remind them what has happened.

4. Discuss the story and see if the child can relate it to their own experience, or perhaps compare it to another story they know.

5. Give praise! Remember that small mistakes need not always be corrected.

If you enjoyed this book, why not try another **TADPOLES** story?